Rhymes

by
Benn Sowerby

Order this book online at www.trafford.com/
or email orders@trafford.com

Most Trafford titles are also available at major online book retailers.

Note for Librarians: A cataloguing record for this book is available from Library
and Archives Canada at www.collectionscanada.ca/amicus/index-e.html

Printed in Victoria, BC, Canada.

ISBN: 978-1-4269-0316-8

*We at Trafford believe that it is the responsibility of us all, as both individuals
and corporations, to make choices that are environmentally and socially sound.
You, in turn, are supporting this responsible conduct each time you purchase a
Trafford book, or make use of our publishing services.*

*Our mission is to efficiently provide the world's finest, most comprehensive
book publishing service, enabling every author to experience success.
To find out how to publish your book, your way, and have it available
worldwide, visit us online at www.trafford.com/*

 www.trafford.com

North America & international
toll-free: 1 888 232 4444 (USA & Canada)
phone: 250 383 6864 ♦ fax: 250 383 6804 ♦ email: info@trafford.com

The United Kingdom & Europe
phone: +44 (0)1865 487 395 ♦ local rate: 0845 230 9601
facsimile: +44 (0)1865 481 507 ♦ email: info.uk@trafford.com

10 9 8 7 6 5 4 3 2 1

by the same author

for Kay

Can you sharpen your wits on a penknife
Or tickle your toes with your teeth,
Pick out the stars with stalactites
And wind them into a wreath?

◆

Somebody sat on a toadstool
Pensively wriggling her toes:
"What happens when puff-balls burst", she says,
"Nobody knows".

The road goes up, the road goes down,
The road winds all about
And we'll be in El Paso tonight I hope
Before the stars go out.

◆

The moon shines bright as we ride west,
The wind blows cold,
And when we started from the east
The sun dripped gold.

The stones lie heavy on the sod,
The scattered moonlit stones,
But light as dust lies that small pile
Of blanched and brittle bones.

◆

The beacon burns on the desert,
The lighthouse shines on the sea,
And my pharos gleams with a little white light
Alone for me.

The day dawns cold,
The wind sings high,
I'm warm in bed
And there I'll lie.

◆

The old white horse
In the green meadow
Canters after
His own shadow,

But when it lengthens
Across the grass
He tires, and, bewildered,
Gives up the race.

A little white ship
Sails over the clouds,
The sunlight golden
In its shrouds,

And it carries your thoughts
Away from me
Where I cannot follow
By land or sea.

Weeds in the water,
Flowers in the grass,
Blue mist of forget-me-nots
In a green looking glass.

Walking to High Button
Up on the hill
I saw the huntsman looking
For a fox to kill.

Coming from High Button
Down the steep hill,
Gay fox away,
They were looking for him still.

◆

Singing in a sampan
On the inland sea
"Wonder where tomorrow
We shall be".

The daises spread their ample shades
For emmets as they pass
Toiling among the twisted blades
Of tall green grass.

The sun has all the skill for which of old
The patient alchemists so vainly yearned:
This evening in the western sky he turned
A leaden cloud to silver, then to gold.

◆

This meadow holds all summer in its scent
Of fresh grreen grass,
And in these cups, when summer's gold is spent,
Hoards a residium of the days that pass.

He says he could not bear his lawn
As the man-over-the-way's is
All cluttered up
With buttercups
And daises.

To him all flowers of natural growth
Are pests, vicious and ugly
In this fallacy
Grown callous he
Roots them up smugly.

Let him enjoy the empty pride
Of horticultural masters
In primulas
Or zinnias
Or asters,

So I have cowslip meadows where
To enjoy sweet-scented hours,
And primroses
In coppices
And frail wildflowers.

We sit and watch the daylight fade
While deeper still the snow is laid,
And if it snows the whole night through
We'll never get to Numazu.

The day like a young girl opens wide her eyes
In admiration and delight
At the rich jewels that the sun displays
Lifting the velvet cover of the night.

◆

The sea and sky are empty as
Along the shore we walk
Save for a lonley cormorant
Two sampans and a hawk.

The feather-green bamboos
Bend in the wind
Bowing the with ceremonious politeness
Of the Japanese.
The frogs croak in the ricefields.

◆

There's always flotsam on the shore,
And if it's not flotsam it's jetsam,
But if there's any valuables
It's never I who gets 'em.

The birds are nesting again,
And the cries of the swift and the gannet
Echo about the cilffs
Of weathered granite.

Above the scuffle, aloof
And unheeding, perches a sparrow
Disdaining the swifts that swoop
To their steep nests straight as an arrow.

◆

Do not teach your child too late
The right way to expectorate.
It is no idle whim!
If he can't spit straight
By the time he's eight
It's a bad look-out for him.

There is no sound now within the house
Close shuttered to the night
Where faintly my fitful candle shows
Its aureole of light.

With soundless steps from room to room
I have searched everywhere
And paused to pierce the sudden gloom
At the well head of the stair.

Although in vain some sign I seek
I feel the prescence near
Of one who either will not speak
Or cannot make me hear,

Another shadow, it may be in fear
Sharing uneasily
This solitude, as dimly aware
As I perhaps, of me.

From my unwinking pharos
I watched the world revolve,
In ivoried seclusion
Freeing my resolve.

Bound tireless in an orbit
Described by rigid laws,
I fancied some great purpose
Uniting aim and cause.

But when I descended
I found it to my grief
Torn and troubled windily
Like an autumn leaf.

◆

From those who shove and push and fight,
From those who shut the windows tight,
From those who sprawl about and snore,
From thos who spit upon the floor,
From those who belch and sniff and cough,
From those who take their garments off,
From those who never cease to eat,
From those who tread upon our feet,
From orange suckers spitting pips,
From those who hawk and smack their lips,
From those who fidget, fuss, and fume,
From those who take up all the room,
From those who stretch and kick our shins,
From all whose countless other sins,
Will reap, we hope, a just reward,
From fellow travellers, Good Lord
deliver us.

A cuckoo call in these far hills,
Recalls the spring in Chiddingfold
Where the bright horde of daffodils
Converts the halfpenny to gold.

◆

In this deserted field of thistles
Now scarcely even a blackbird whistles,
But soon, when summer days grow late,
The long-tailed tits will congregate
again: then here there'll be enough
Small acrobats of light winged fluff,
Cheeping and fluttering, to cap
Each purple swaying thistle top.

◆

I looked for Good, but Evil
Answered my call,
Jealousy, lost friendship,
And a spent light growing small.

I had no enemies to spoil
The fields on which I spent my toil,
But one who shared in them destroyed
The simple pleasures I enjoyed,
Insidiously sowed a doubt -
Alas! I could not root it out, -
And then it grew before my eyes
And daily still it multiplies.
It choked my green and tender seed
With its rank overgrowth of weed;
But when I thought to leave the grain
And dig all up and sow again
The tangled roots had then so bound
The earth and tunnelled all the ground
I could not break the soil or thrust
My spade beneath the solid crust.
And still it grows and spreads unchecked
Over the harvest that it wrecked.
Now very soon it will provide
A thicket dense enough to hide
My grief, and men will envy me
When in a little while they see
Shoots of my rank and bitter weed
Become at last a wood indeed.

The trees sweep by starred with small white faces
And I cannot tell whether they are flowers or faded
leaves.

I would have whiteness for a dream to be
Continually
Lapping the mind,
The surging power of the resistless sea
And its tranquility
Smoothing the sand,
The unyielding instinct of the proud gulls high
And dauntless cry
Feeling the wind.

◆

Nothing soothes so as the sound of rain
Over low hedgerows where the mist clings close,
When but for its light murmurous monotone
And the earth's drinking all sounds faint and cease.

Let us forget. Pretence grows troublesome
When it no longer has power to deceive.
We have dwelt too long with unreality
And truth is urgent: we must take our leave.

Let us forget the dreams and the illusions,
Days of rare beauty, nights of long content.
Life has no more like these to offer us.
The lamp is worthless when the oil is spent.
Let us forget.

O, to be out again with the lark under a clear sky
As though we were in the same universe together,
He singing and I
Listening,
Hearing the excultant song of a new life
In the fluttering shrill notes
He utters so breathlessly.

◆

If there was sorrow when the world was young
How is it now the world is old?
All sad songs were ever sung,
All sad tales were ever told
Cannot match with bitter tears
The drifted litter of the years.

He who carries the sod in his pocket
Stares out of an eyeless socket.
If the sod cleaves to your feet
You will fear neither cold nor heat:
But he who bears the sod in his heart
Lives a life apart.

"Life" said Alcnin "is a tendency
"To be
"A flea".
But I
Want to try
To be a fly
Hi-tiddle-y-i.

Sadly now the wind grieves
Plucking at the bamboo leaves.
This way and that they sidle by
As if uncertain where to lie,
But fall eventually they must
And print their zebra stripes in dust.

Unwilling murderers daily still
At every step we crush and kill
The little life of simple things
With fragile legs and filmy wings.

Poor fly, you found your final night
By candle light
Eyes dazzle-charmed
From safety shadow-fringed
Till with wings singed
Submerged in seas
Of candle grease
You lay embalmed

◆

In black, prescribed for those interred,
With dutifully heaving bust,
Please don't come here to disturb
These unreluctant grains of dust,

For you' re well rid of me at last,
Tucked snugly in for worm's delight,
And I'm well rid of life who cast
My net for stars and drew in night.

I never see an elephant
But tears come to my eyes
For such a tiny intellect
In such a monstrous size.

I never see an elephant
But tears come to my eyes
For all the things he cannot do
That make a man so wise.

He cannot do arithmetic,
Decline a latin noun,
Or give the French for artichoke,
Or wear a cap and gown.

How sad to be an elephant
With nothing else to do
But eat and sleep and play about
Or else live in a zoo.